I0748453

PRAISE FOR CHAIM FREIBERG

"When I read his stories, I am welcomed into the lovely world of Mr. Freiberg which he creates with vivid imagery and engaging storytelling."
Lydia Bailey

"One of the most resilient and talented persons I know"
Dr. Shulamit Mor
Department of Psychology, York University, Toronto

"Timeless tales of beauty and nature."
Teuta Pilana, concert pianist, professor of piano, Long Island University, New York.

"Stories that inspire hope and love"
Stephanie Siefken, Award winning artist and author, St Petersburg, Florida

---

"Chaim Freiberg paints a beautiful picture of life as he sees and feels it"
Billie Stewart, Calhoon Band

Lily Flowers Finds Love

and other tales of passion

This is a work of fiction. Names, characters, businesses, places, events, locales, and incidents are either the products of the author's imagination or used in a fictitious manner. Any resemblance to actual persons, living or dead, or actual events is purely coincidental.

Published by St. Petersburg Press
St. Petersburg, FL
www.stpetersburgpress.com

Design and composition by St. Petersburg Press and Isa Crosta
Cover design by St. Petersburg Press and Isa Crosta

Hardcover ISBN: 978-1-940300-69-6
eBook ISBN: 978-1-940300-70-2

First Edition

Lily Flowers Finds Love
and other tales of passion

BY CHAIM FREIBERG
ILLUSTRATIONS BY SAYLOR PASCOE

The author would like to thank Theresa Scott, Joshua Kizivat, Chester Sudzinski and Amy Cianci for their support and valuable editorial suggestions.

Curtain Call

The shouts of "*Brava, Brava*!" were deafening
The Diva was taking it all in.
Standing near the stage I realized
she was not as young as she seemed
from the last row and
what I thought from the distance
to be glittering diamonds
on her neck
were really large drops
from a river of hot sweat
glowing in the limelight.
my heart went out to her and
as I wept,
how I wished she would remain
my young and innocent Gilda –
Forever
She left the exit door unnoticed
and alone
only to return the next day
to her real life
On the stage

By Chaim Freiberg

Table of contents

The Opera House In The Heights

Premiered in 1850, Verdi's Rigoletto tells the dramatic tale of a young duke of untrustworthy character who seduces the innocent Gilda, and the tragic outcome that results when her father, the jester Rigoletto, seeks revenge.

The days of the Gold Rush were over but the Opera House, built of limestone and brick and reachable by a walk up on the cobblestone winding street, was still standing tall on top of the windswept hill in the town of Mountain Hawk, Colorado. Time had taken its toll on the appearance of the tenacious and strong building, but its nobility and beauty had endured the ravages of neglect and weather. An architectural gem, the theatre was erected in the late 1800's by the newly wealthy citizens of Mountain Hawk who wished to continue their long European tradition of opera performances. The theatre was designed and built in the Renaissance Revival style, and over time, the jewel box Opera House had become known as "The Opera House in the Heights."

With the decline of the Gold Rush, the once prosperous mining town in the West was now mostly abandoned by the fortune-seeking residents who had all left for far more profitable destinations. Occasional passing travelers, intrigued by the ghostly air of the deserted town, stopped by to experience the thrilling sensation of bygone days that permeated the small and empty streets. The charming Victorian Opera Inn on Main Street was, until she died, still run by the old, Irish born, Mrs. Gallagher. She loved to tell stories, over Irish cider, about the Opera House's early days and the glorious evenings when elegant couples had arrived at the inn on horse-drawn fancy carriages and sat on its porch for tea and pastries before leisurely walking up the hill to the Opera House.

Nowadays, the two large Palladian windows above the entrance doors to the theatre appear like two otherworldly old faces, suspiciously studying any passerby walking under the night shadow of the old building, with the stone carved inscription that reads "Opera House." The ornate street gaslight lamp at its entrance is still lit every evening as it was on the day of the last performance in the Opera House. It was rumored amongst opera lovers that in the past, when the Opera House keeper was still alive, pale light streamed softly through the windows of the aging building, along with distant sounding echoes of "Caro Nome" ("Dearest Name"), Gilda's famously intricate and exquisite aria, as sang by Leila Ponce in her last performance at the Opera House. One can see the announcement of the 1910 performance of Rigoletto

still mounted on the front wall, all faded but, even now, readable. It illustrates the image of the captivating soprano who, years back, had created a sensation when at 18 years of age, she had first appeared as Gilda, on the stage of the illustrious Grand Opera House in her native South American city. Since then, audiences were entranced with Leila Ponce's striking beauty and talent to match. She was endlessly adored and admired by her fans who were willing to travel any distance, no matter how far, to hear her bell-like soprano, glittering like pearls in the silvery moonlight.

It was in 1910, twenty years after her debut, that thirty-eight year old Leila was now, after having sang in major cities of the world, on her way to the little town of Mountain Hawk. In her signature role, she was still the image of the young and ethereal figure of Gilda, with ripples of blond hair and dressed in a long white nightgown, as the story goes.

Leila arrived in Mountain Hawk three days before her first appearance of the opera season. One special car of the train was carrying her trunks, containing the elaborate costumes and her personal evening gowns specially sewn to delineate her lithe figure and match her exotic complexion. A luxurious Motorwagen was sent to fetch her from the train station and a specially appointed room at the Opera Inn was prepared for her. Upon meeting the other cast members on the following day's rehearsal, Leila was gracious and formal at once. The slight foreign accent one detected in her rich speaking voice added to her aura of distant and cosmopolitan sophistication and was additionally enhanced by the whispering hint of a delicate French perfume she was wearing. At the end of the day's rehearsals, Leila retired to her room at the inn. She made sure to get her night's rest in anticipation of the next day's final and full voiced dress rehearsal to be led by the young orchestra conductor who had arrived from Chicago days earlier to prepare the orchestra. The day of opening night, Leila spent, as she always had, in seclusion. She studied her role and did some easy and soothing exercises to keep her voice warm and supple.

The theatre was ready for the opening night performance: Flowers were placed in the entrance hall, delicate confections were tastefully arranged at the refreshments bar and Leila Ponce's dressing room was ready to meet every possible wish of a queen. It had all been prepared by the odd, long-faced young man known in Mountain Hawk as "Jonah of The Opera House."

Two years earlier, on a windy afternoon, he showed up in Mountain Hawk, a young lad and a stranger in the town. Mr. Gallagher and his wife Lavinia, the kind and childless Irish innkeepers, asked him no questions as they took him in and offered him a home in exchange for help. For as long as they knew him, he had never been heard speaking. It was finally presumed that he was mute and was given the name Jonah. While he never spoke, his wide-opened innocent eyes told the story of his soul. When the great and larger-than-life diva Victoria Ferrari stayed at the inn, Jonah was found laying on the floor outside her door, tears coming down his face upon listening to her singing Violetta's "Addio, del Passato" ("Farewell to the Past"). Mr. Gallagher, knowing the Opera House's manager, recommended that Jonah would be hired as the theatre's night guard and stage hand. Jonah lived in the Opera House ever since. His dwelling was the tiny attic high above the stage, reached by a climb on the tall wall-ladder leading to the scenery-holding catwalk. He always looked out the window when singers arrived at the Opera House for the new season. By now, probably 18-year-old Jonah knew, after seeing Leila Ponce, that for him, she was the one and only. He stood still for a while and then climbed to his attic, buried his face in his hands, tears flowing from his eyes, and his heart a river of emotions. Leila was the one he had been waiting for. He found her at the remote Opera House in the Heights.

Opening night was expected to be an exciting musical and social event. Rigoletto was to be performed on three consecutive nights. On the first night, Leila sang gloriously and her execution of the "Caro Nome" coloratura was later described by the press as "miraculous," but back at her dressing room Leila was not happy. She was the only one to know that, for the very first time, she missed the high C Sharp, the highest note required for that aria, and one which she had never missed before. To the disappointment of her fans, she declined to receive visitors as was customary. She wanted to be alone.

Sitting at her dresser, she studied herself in the mirror, wondering whether she was getting too old for the role. Suddenly, she was startled to see the reflection of a young man at the door, standing, boyishly shy and manly at once. As he came in, Leila felt a sudden light and unfamiliar quiver through her body. "He must be half my age, and I am irresistibly attracted to him," she heard her inner voice telling her. She was intoxicated by the magnetic power that his close vicinity had over her and felt her heart palpitating faster. They locked eyes through the mirror. Slowly wiping off her makeup she left her painted lips bloody red. As he came close, she turned her head towards him, closed her eyes and surrendered as she felt his full and soft lips meeting hers. She no longer agonized over the lost C Sharp. It was perfectly in place in the following two performances, after which Jonah, ending his years long silence, promised her that her "Caro Nome" will forever be the only one to be heard at the Opera House in The Heights.

Leila Ponce never left Mountain Hawk. She chose to stay for a simpler life with Jonah, fulfilling the passion she could previously live only on the stage.

Years later Jonah was an old man, and Leila had become a haunting legend of the past. At the time when Leila came to Mountain Hawk in 1910, the newly invented gramophone was sent to the Opera House as a gift from a wealthy patron. Jonah had kept it, and unbeknownst to Leila, recorded the perfect execution of her last performance. For as long as he lived, to his very last day at age 98, Jonah played her "Caro Nome" every night, faithfully keeping his promise as her beautiful voice was heard every midnight in Mountain Hawk: a remembrance of the beloved, one and only, Leila Ponce.

LILY FLOWERS FINDS LOVE

Completed in 1902, Claude Debussy's Pelleas and Melisande tells the story of the mysterious Melisande found alone in the forest by a man named Golaud. After marrying him she meets his younger brother Pelleas, and the two fall in love as their tragic fate inevitably takes hold.

On a rainy New York afternoon, a tall and elegant woman stood in front of the formidable building made of granite and limestone. It was the newly built Opera House on 34th street which was owned and run by Leon Goldstern, the adventurous and enterprising impresario who championed newly composed operas. The theatre's enormous stage was planned with the vision to be a venue for the productions in the new style of Theatrical Realism and the worthy setting in which to feature Mr. Goldstern's favorite and exclusive opera star, the auburn-haired and exquisitely flamboyant

Lily Flowers. She was now closely studying in detail the large publicity poster announcing her much heralded performance in the premier of *Aeneas and Amelie*, the new opera that had been composed, at Mr. Godstern's request, by a rising young French composer. The artful drawing on the poster portrayed her as a willowy maiden, her long golden colored hair flowing in the breeze, and an air of youthful innocence about her.

Lily had personally been asked by Mr. Goldstern to sing the role of Amelie at the opening of the new season at his New York Opera House. The opera's program notes read: "Amelie is a young woman who is found inexplicably lost in the streets of a big city and is rescued by a young passerby named Darius. Mystified by her beauty, he instantly falls in love with her. Bringing her to his father's vineyard estate in the Upper Hudson valley, he marries her. The two live under the watchful eye of Achilles, Darius' domineering father who is initially suspicious of the young and enigmatic woman's motives. There, Amelie meets Darius' half-brother, the young and gentle Aeneas and the two are attracted to each other. The opera ends as the love triangle leads to a tragic ending." Having had studied the role meticulously, Lily was thoroughly prepared for the evening's performance, as she had always been with every detail of her career. Diligently acquired through the years she had been living in Paris, her French diction was impeccable and her understanding of the French nuances qualified her as the natural choice to sing the role of the fragile Amelie. She was ready to conquer the critics and the audiences of New York.

Lily Flowers had made a name for herself in the opera-world after having been hailed by the French critics as the "Sarah Bernhard of the Lyric Stage." In addition, she was

a woman of chic and elegance and her discriminating taste belied the hardship she had experienced in her childhood.

As long as she remembered herself, Lily had perpetually been driven by a burning and insatiable ambition to be the best in anything she had set her mind on. She was intent on becoming an acclaimed opera singer and earned it earnestly through hard and methodical work. With that in mind, she was highly disciplined and could, at times, be cold and calculating.

A precocious and only child growing up in a rural dairy farmhouse in Scotland, her stage talent was evident early through her singing and acting in her school plays where the kind music teacher, seeing her potential, offered her free singing lessons. Lily's mother was determined to make her own unfulfilled dreams come true through Lily's fame. She left her husband behind and, with the little money she saved, bought a passage in lower deck steerage on a cargo ship leaving from Liverpool. Two weeks later, mother and daughter arrived in Chicago, the American musical capital at the time. There, through the services of the St. Margaret of Scotland Parish, they found shelter in "Haven For Women," a Catholic charity home. Soon enough, mother found employment doing housekeeping and cooking while Lily's undeniable talent and self-assurance, along with her mother's persistence, brought her, now 15 years old, the attention of the theatre managers and musical directors who engaged her to sing and act in the many new regional Opera Houses that had been built in smaller towns. After a run of performances across the continent, mother took daughter Lily, now 18 years of age, to Paris for the training they both knew she needed for the level of singing expected to achieve the international career and recognition they were seeking. They traveled to Paris, the world's music capital, where Lily auditioned and was accepted as a full scholarship student at the famed Conservatory to study with Mme. Edith Charbonnet de Phillip, a former leading soprano of the Paris Opera who had become a respected and influential teacher.

A known celebrity, Lily was thirty-four years old and alone, now that her mother was gone, crossing the ocean on board the luxurious SS Normandie. She was on her way to New York City to star as Amelie at the Opera House on 34th street.

Opening night's performance of *Aeneas and Amelie* was a great musical and social event in the city of New York. With much publicity and newspaper columns speculating about the private life of Lily Flowers, Mr. Goldstern's Opera House was the place to be that night. His Opera House on 34th street had already become a source of concern for the long-established and prestigious Opera House further uptown which had lost many audiences who preferred the more contemporary shows at Mr. Goldstern's New York Opera House. In addition, Lily had a particular interest, secretly held, in the evening's success as she was holding a personal resentment towards the other Opera House for not ever having offered her an invitation to appear on its stage. She was bent, in order to appease her wounded pride, to be in the position to turn it down should such an invitation be extended to her in the future. She was able, however, the consummate artist that she was, to set all these thoughts and considerations aside once she was in her stage role. *Aeneas and Amelie* was hailed as a great opera and her performance was described in the press as an "artistic triumph." She was crowned by the music critics as the greatest singing actress of the day.

Following the roaring applause, Lily was back at her dressing room. Gracefully, but firmly, she declined an invitation to celebrate her success at a private party to be taking place at the official residence of the French cultural attaché with the French Ambassador and other notables in attendance. Her vocal care and general well-being were her utmost priority. Always remembering Mme. Charbonnet's wise advice, Lily Flowers made sure to get proper rest in order to be in shape for the physical demands of the next day's performance. Her career and on-stage success were all that mattered to her.

Alone in her dressing room, Lily carefully removed her heavy makeup with a hydrating mask made of a secret formula of natural oils, personally prepared for her by a pharmacist in Paris. She was a woman particular in every detail of her life on, as well as off, the stage. Ready to leave the theatre, she changed to street clothes and covering her head with a sizable Parisian cloche hat, unrecognized, easily eluded the waiting fans standing outside the stage door and was intent on reaching her hotel, the nearby Astor, as quickly as possible.

Walking out into the busy street, meaning to avoid the heavy traffic and the fumes coming from the vehicles, Lily took a turn and, as she kept walking, lost in her thoughts, found herself in a small and dark alley. She could not help, with some wry irony, think of Amelie, the frightened and confused young woman she played on stage just an hour ago. Leaning on a pole of a dimly lit street-lamp and trying to collect herself, she could hear her own heartbeat pounding in her chest. Lily Flowers felt, for the very first time ever perhaps, frightened and insecure. From the distance through the darkness, discern a human figure moving towards her. She did not have enough time to examine whether she was anxious or relieved before hearing the friendly and fresh voice of a young man: "You seem to be lost, can I help?" he asked. "I need to get to the Hotel Astor," she replied, and in a girlish intonation she never knew she had, added: "I am lost." He was close and she could feel his warm breath on her face. "There is something comforting about it," she surprisingly found herself thinking. Catching sight of his face, she presumed him to be in his twenties. Without a word, he offered her his arm. Lily felt its muscular strength and was fully aware and honest to admit to herself that she did not care where they were heading, as long as the moment would last forever.

Arriving at the hotel's brightly lit entrance, Lily saw the young man's face clearly and wanted to remember every detail of it. Her heart skipped a beat as he left with a gentle smile under his velvety mustache. They both turned their heads to see each other once more. Entering her hotel suite, Lily was walking on air and the fragrance of the roses on her dresser filled her with a new sense of freedom she was not able to identify. She was enthralled by a newfound and captivating call for liberation.

The next evening Lily was Amelie again on the great stage of the New York Opera House. From the front of the stage, taking her bows, she recognized a young man's face. With the thousands applauding her, that was all she saw. Their eyes met. He waited for her outside the stage door in the rain and he was holding an open umbrella.

The next day, the review of her performance read: "The great Lily Flowers sang with sublime beauty as there was new softness and warmth in her voice. She let go of her familiar steely vocal control and allowed her heart to sing instead." At last, Lily Flowers found love.

LUCIA IN THE BELL TOWER

Premiered in 1835, Donizetti's Lucia Di Lammermoor tells the story of the fragile Lucia who loses her mind and commits a crime when she is forced by her brother to marry a man she does not love.

It was in the summer of 1958 when the young American couple were enjoying their honeymoon in the picturesque countryside of Scotland. The splendid weather, the clear blue sky and the fresh air in the Highlands created an ideal setting for their celebration. The charming chalet they stayed in was on the grounds of the venerable castle, which years ago, had been the formal residence for the wealthy Acheson dynasty. After an elegant, candlelit dinner in the dining room at the quaint West Hill Village-Inn nearby, they sat at the ornate gazebo in the midst of the lilac garden by the small pond, watching the swans sail by. The formidable and moody old castle, painted by the silvery glow of the moon, was seen standing across on the steep and rocky hill, looking like a fortress, a timeless monument of the past, towering over the village below.

The young couple had made plans to attend the following day's opening night performance of *LUCIA DI LAMMERMOOR* at the charming old theatre, the Amelia Duncan Opera House, which was gently nestled amidst Scots Pines and Birch trees at the foot of the hill. The many opera lovers, from near and far away, came to hear the superb singing in the memorable theatre that had recently been reopened after it had been closed for many years following an unfinished performance of *Lucia Di Lammermoor* in 1904. Shadows of the past were still hovering in its phantasmal ambience. The strong presence of Amelia Duncan, a woman of classic beauty and regal deportment, was still domineering the space from the oil-painted portrait mounted high above the entrance to the auditorium, facing each audience member as they entered through the door.

The theatre was built in 1901 by the affluent and charitable Sir Ronald Duncan who commissioned the renowned English architect Alistair Burton to design it in the plush Edwardian style. It was a gift from Mr. Duncan to his beloved wife Amelia, a woman of dramatic presence and a brilliant operatic voice. On its stage, Amelia Duncan was destined to be the reigning star. The intimate auditorium was designed to meet the distinct expectations of the high-ranking members of society and wealthy patrons of the arts. Amelia's dressing room was imbued with the delicate fragrance of lilac flowers and was furnished with every possible luxury and comfort. Amelia's stage-costumes, as well as her real-life wardrobe, were custom tailored for her by the elite couturiers of the Augustus House of Fashion in London, and made of exquisite fabrics imported from the Far East. Her personal attendant and confidante, Nina, prepared her to go on stage looking the very real heroine she was about to portray.

At the time, Amelia Duncan distinguished herself in the role of Lucia di Lammermoor in the opera by that same name. It was a role that allowed her to exhibit her theatrical genius and her breathtaking execution of the strikingly arresting Mad Scene when, emerging from her wedding night bedroom, the tragic Lucia walks down the staircase, her wedding gown covered with blood. She electrified the audience with her brilliant and authentic depiction of a woman on the brink of insanity, hallucinating and hearing imaginary voices.

As the young American couple joined the dressed up ticket holders making their way to the Opera House, the winding path was lit with old style, vintage gas lamps. The newly married young couple was about to experience their first night at the opera. Cast as Lucia was Dame Alma Smith, an English opera singer who was already known for her dramatic and vocal talents and was engaged to sing at the prestigious Opera House in Chicago the following year. Her appearance at the Amelia Duncan Opera House in West Hill was anticipated with great interest as it was her debut in the role of Lucia. Influential critics of important newspapers arrived to cover the event. Her Mad Scene created a sensation that won her a standing ovation. A festive post-performance reception was arranged beforehand to honor and celebrate her successful appearance. Elegant tables were set on the grounds, with caramel shortbread and delightful Victorian ices served. A toast was raised by the conductor to honor the celebrated artist, Dame Alma Smith, on her portrayal of Lucia. When the young couple headed back to their cottage, the time was close to midnight. Still entranced by their new and thrilling experience at the opera and attracted by the mysterious allure of the old castle in the distance, they took a moonlit walk up the hill.

When they were near the castle they were struck by the sight of a woman dressed in white. Appearing gaunt and unworldly, she stood at the top of the tower. Holding a lantern, her long white hair was flowing in the light breeze. She suddenly disappeared out of sight, but then, the flickering light from the lantern indicated she was descending the tower's spiral staircase.

The young couple was beguiled and sorry at once for the odd figure they had just seen. With some effort they managed to open the heavy wooden entrance door to the tower. There stood, motionless, the enigmatic woman, the very image of an ethereal, almost transparent apparition, staring at them intensely and inquisitively. The young couple could tell that in the past she possessed rare beauty. After standing still and silent, she suddenly turned around and slowly walked up the stairs, barely touching the ground.

When the couple left, they turned their heads up to the top of the tower to see the woman in white once again, standing and gazing at some distant place, a faint, obscure smile on her thin lips.

The next morning the young couple, intrigued, inquired with Mr. Campbell, the old and tight-lipped innkeeper, about the identity of the mysterious woman they had seen the previous night. Mr. Campbell seemed ill at ease with their inquiry. Declining to discuss her and looking down, he said that he knew nothing about her. However, while serving them breakfast and having had overheard the conversation, Mrs. Bailey,

the Irish lady-cook of the inn, her arms resting on her ample hips, bent over the table and whispered to them: "The woman you saw in the tower is Elspeth Duncan, granddaughter of the late Amelia Duncan, the great opera singer who sang her last performance in 1904. That night, after concluding her brilliant interpretation of the Mad Scene, she suddenly stood motionless on the stage, staring at somewhere in the unknown distance and unable to finish her performance. The audience left as she was carried away from the stage and was never seen in public again. Following the order of her husband, Mr. Sutherland, the Opera House closed its doors since. The woman you have seen in the tower is Elspeth, Amelia's granddaughter. As she grew to be a young woman, her beauty resembled that of her grandmother, Amelia. When, after the war, she met and fell in love with a young Irish soldier, her father forbade her from marrying him, a man of a humble, working-class family. Heartbroken, she was forced to enter a marriage to a wealthy older man she did not love. He died on their wedding night. Amid rumors that he was poisoned, Elspeth, to save her life, was pronounced insane and was committed to spend the rest of her life alone in the castle's bell tower."

Upon hearing the strange and tragic parallel between Lucia's and Elspeth's stories, the couple was moved to tears. They believed that seeing Lucia live on stage, would have a healing effect on Elspeth's bewildered mind. The last performance was already sold out, but upon learning of Elspeth's identity, three special seats were placed, concealed by the curtain at the very edge of the stage. The young couple assured the management and authorities that they would be responsible for her safety and for those in the audience, as well as for those performing on the stage. Attending the performance, Elspeth wore that same white wedding gown she had the night they first saw her. She looked like a dreamy apparition, delicate and radiant.

Throughout the performance, Elspeth focused on the riveting drama on the stage and seemed to study each and every gesture of Alma Smith. When the flute was heard playing the faint and distant sounding opening notes of the Mad Scene, Elspeth looked transfixed. At the end of the Mad Scene, as the audience was applauding with enthusiasm, she closed her eyes, leaned on the back of her seat as tears were streaming down her face.

When the opera was finished and the audience had left, Elspeth was taken backstage to be introduced to Alma Smith who was in awe having had heard of her grandmother, Amelia Duncan and her acclaimed Lucia. Alma Smith looked closely at Elspeth's face and exclaimed admiringly: "You ARE Lucia!" Elspeth smiled. Thoughtfully and deliberately, she replied: "Throughout my life I have been consumed and haunted by the ghosts of Lucia and Amelia Duncan, but tonight I have broken the chain and have freed myself, choosing to be me, and I do wish you all the best." She then turned to the young American couple and, with a confident sounding voice, said: "Let's go."

Elspeth accepted the young couple's invitation to return with them to Boston. She became the loving Nanny to their future twin children and stayed with them as long as she lived.

THE DIVINE SISTER ANGELICA

Premiered in 1854, Verdi's La Traviata tells the story of Violetta, a beautiful and pure-hearted courtesan, who gives up material riches and sacrifices her own happiness for the sake of the one man she truly loves.

The Opera House stood on a cliff overlooking the bay and the emerald colored sea stretching far into the horizon and beyond. For many years the theatre had its doors closed as echoes of past and unresolved mystery were still wavering in its empty space.

The theatre was erected in 1893 according to the plan of Diego Antonio, the renowned Spanish architect. It was built at the request of the Crown and the island's governing council. Its mission was to enhance the "savoire-faire" and social graces of the officials and the diplomats often visiting the island for political missions or business affairs. It also served as a venue in which Western culture was introduced to the colonial island's natives who proudly called the theatre: "Our Opera House."

On performance nights, the theatre's facade was illuminated by powerful gas-lamps revealing an artfully painted large poster mounted above the majestic Corinthian columns, depicting the opera's main characters. The Plaza de Paz, with the ornate water fountain in its center, was vibrantly animated with the exuberant audience waiting for the bell-ringing, signaling that it was time to enter the theatre. Pictures of the European governing capital were painted on the walls of the entrance lobby, adding an air of worldly elegance. The marble grand staircase led into an auditorium of ravishing splendor. Above the floor level were three tiers of balconies and private side-boxes. The gold and crystal chandelier hanging from the domed ceiling washed the auditorium with dazzling light, adjusted to the desired effect. The seats were luxuriously cushioned with red velvet and the stage front-curtain was deep night blue, glowing with a touch of silver, much like the changing colors of the sea surrounding the island and the starry sky above it. The names of the great opera composers were imprinted in gold leaf above the stage.

On that memorable night, the air was infused with an exquisite blend of exotic perfumes as well as whispers and hushed conversations relating to Esperanza Renato, the glamorous and acclaimed star about to sing the leading role of Violetta in Verdi's *La Traviata*. At the conclusion of her memorable performance that night, Esperanza Renato left the stage forever.

Covered with a black veil, she hurriedly exited the stage door where a carriage had already been waiting for her. A short note she had left in her dressing room read, that much to her regret, she was compelled to cancel all her future engagements and had no plans to be seen or heard on the opera stage ever again. Her sudden and abrupt departure was a great source of disappointment and sadness to all her admirers and all those who were hoping to hear her in the future. As time passed, rumors abounded on the nature of her sudden disappearance and where she had possibly gone to, but it all remained unanswered. Known to have previously been living alone in a secluded villa near the Mediterranean coast, it was assumed and hoped for that she would eventually be seen again, but her whereabouts remained unknown. Few knew that the famous and fabulous opera star Esperanza Renato was an orphan, and as a child had endured poverty and hunger.

Years have passed and the name Esperanza Renato has become a myth. The Opera House in the island had never recovered from her sudden and unexplained disappearance. The theatre won a ghostly reputation and opera sopranos declined offers to appear on its stage for fear of her shadowy fate. The doors were shut with no future plans until, in the course of time, the island gained autonomy and a new generation replaced the island's old colonial council.

It was voted by the new council that the Opera House will open its doors again so that its old and dusty stage be put to a purposeful mission. It was hoped that the theatre will be reborn and come alive again with a performance by the children's choir of the nearby orphanage, where many parentless children had found a warm home, and were cared for by compassionate nuns.

The concert took place on a Sunday afternoon. The children were on stage and the music director took her seat at the freshly-tuned piano. Music was about to be heard again in the beloved Opera House.

As the audience fell into silence, a tall and noble figure walked slowly towards the center of the stage. She was known to all as Sister Angelica. Her past life was unknown to anyone in the convent. As she lowered her face down in prayer, the choir sang the introduction to her solo. The voice that filled the auditorium brought back memories of past greatness. It was the sublime voice that was heard singing Traviata's "Addio del Passato" ("Farewell to the Past") at the Opera House years ago, just before it was shut. It was now the heavenly voice of the divine Sister Angelica singing "Casta Diva": The prayer of the High Priestess to the goddess of chastity.

PAGLIACCI IN DEATH VALLEY, NEVADA

Premiered in 1892, Ruggero Leoncavallo's Pagliacci is a drama about an acting troupe led by a man who, out of jealousy, is ultimately driven to murder his actress wife and her lover.

It all happened in 1898 when many silver mining camps had already appeared on the map and grew to become small towns with families, schools and the communal life which included culture and entertainment. It was the high time of the Silver Boom.

One such town was Hornsilver, the destination towards which three prairie wagons were, as a caravan, ploddingly making their way in the darkness on the dry, crusty soil of the desert. The wooden, steel-rimmed wheels rattled in constant ramble, sounding like a weary moan in the stillness, echoing the pace of the old and overworked horses, stoic and resigned, were lamentfully dragging the wagons. The dark sky and the unchanging scenery of the stark landscape were the bleak backdrop for the languid and strange apparition, resembling a somber procession under the pale, gloomy blue-white moonlight. From time to time, an achingly melancholic melody could be heard in the midst of the stillness, the soulful singing telling of yearnings and longings, unfulfilled.

The wagons were carrying the sets, costumes and the small group of singing actors belonging to a traveling theatrical troupe called "Amorosa." They traveled from town to town, performing before the hard-working townspeople who were in need of a respite from the harsh desert living conditions. An outdoor entertainment in the cool night air always afforded a refreshing relief to their bodies and minds. The troupe were now on their way to Hornsilver, the booming mining town near the county of Esmeralda in Nevada.

They arrived at Hornsilver before the break of day and a cheerful trumpet tune, followed by a drum roll, heard through the little town, announced their arrival. That day, everyone was allowed to leave work early so they could to be on time for the show. The improvised stage and the sets were all ready for the evening's show. The entrance fee was collected as the excited audience arrived. Some brought along chairs and some sat on the ground covered with blankets to keep themselves warm in the chilly night air. Signor Ruggiero Sanguini, the owner and director of the troupe, came on stage and announced through a large and colorful paper cone, the evening's show: *The Clowns*; Cynically masked as an amusing entertainment, it really is a dramatic tale of love, betrayal and death, in the Old Italian style of the *Commedia de'll Arte*. It centers on its main characters, husband and wife, Pagliaccio and Colombina, both costumed as clowns. The end of the play caught the startled audience in sudden suspense and an unpredicted surprise as they had not expected clowns to experience human tragedy. The audience returned home subdued and perplexed while the troupe was in a hurry to load their sets and feed the horses. They were ready to start the overnight journey to their next destination. There, they would repeat their performance to earn their meager livelihood.

After counting the revenue from the performance, and paying each performer their share, Signor Sanguini headed towards the wagon he shared with his young wife Allegra. When he was near the wagons, he overheard her voice whispering: "When we reach Reno, we'll escape." She was speaking to Francesco, the dark and handsome new member of the troupe who played the young lover with whom, as Colombina, she was having a secret affair on the stage. Upon hearing her words, Signor Sanguini, freezing and turning dead pale, felt like a knife went through his chest.

The troupe mounted their wagons and went on their journey wordlessly, followed by their own looming dark shadows created by the moon's gloomy cold light, while each tall cactus plant on the way appeared as a foreboding cross on a grave. At the first light of dawn, they stopped and ate their breakfast.

Ruggiero Sanguini's heart was laden with deep sorrow. He ate silently, but within his chest, he could hear the anguished scream of a wounded animal. Back at their wagon's coachbox, on their way to the next dusty town, Ruggiero Sanguini suddenly and without turning his head, said to his wife: "We need to rehearse the play's end one last time." Allegra found it odd and sensed a strange fear creeping into her heart. Without

AMOROSA

questioning and with a deceivingly light-hearted tone of voice, she did her best to conceal that fear and with some effort managed to sing Colombina's flirtatious song that preceded the dialogue with Pagliaccio. Mr. Sanguini continued with his script but sounded increasingly testier and alarmingly more short-tempered then when he was acting on the stage. When Allegra, playing the onstage Colombina, continued to coyly evade his confrontational questioning, Ruggiero Sanguini lost his reason and pulled out of his pocket the small knife he kept for protection against bandit attacks during their travel as his wife opened her eyes wide in disbelief. Moments later she was dead.

Members of the troupe buried her next to a Joshua tree to mark her grave. In the blinding light of the desolate landscape, they saw the Winecup flowers turning red as blood and the sun suddenly hid behind a dark cloud. Rain came down in God forsaken Death Valley like teardrops from heaven, washing the blood and purifying the earth. Disconsolate and irredeemable, the troupe left as a flock of watchful black ravens followed them, their ominous croaking chillingly audible throughout the barren and merciless desert while one lone coyote stayed behind, mournfully wailing and howling till they disappeared in the colorless horizon as they were on their way to their next performance.

SYBIL AT THE FRENCH OPERA HOUSE IN LOUISIANA

Composed in 1892, Giacomo Puccini's Manon Lescaux tells the story of the young Manon who is initially driven by vanity to seek riches and ends up dying in the arms of her true love in the wilderness of the Louisiana coast.

At the corner of Bourbon and Toulouse streets near the French Quarter stood a magnificent building. An edifice of grand proportions, it was the Opera House erected in 1859 as a tribute to the high-minded and cultivated taste of the immigrants who had earlier settled in the southern port city they originally called "La Nouvelle Orleans" in the state of Louisiana. A performance at the "Teatre de L'Opera," as it was fondly called by the town's French speaking residents, was attended by the newly affluent families of French descent, as well as the educated and music-loving Creole residents. It was an exciting social event featuring a dazzling display of the latest style of evening gowns created in Paris.

The sumptuous building was commissioned and financed by a wealthy Frenchman who had left Paris years ago to start a new life in Louisiana, following the sudden death of his wife, shortly after her promising debut on the opera stage. To honor her memory, he provided the funds necessary to construct a new theatre that would be an architectural masterpiece, opulent and grand, in the American city known as the "Paris of the South." The expansive stage was equipped with the most up to date technology and made suitable to accommodate the most spectacular productions. The gold curtain featured scenes from known operas and a splendid gold and crystal chandelier imported from Lalique in the French region of Alsace, revealed the harmonious proportions and the eye-pleasing colors of the theatre's interior design.

The announcement that Sybil Sandstrom had accepted the invitation to sing the leading role in *Manon Lescaut* created a great deal of frenzy among the town's opera lovers, all seeking to secure their tickets for her performances. Sybil became the talk of the town.

Born in the American West into the wealthy, well connected Sandstorm family, her musical talent had shown itself early on when at church she was heard, at age five, singing the "Ave Maria" in perfect pitch, along with the choir's soloist. She studied the piano diligently and expressed her interest in making music her lifelong career.

At the age of fifteen Sybil was sent, with her family's consent, along with a chaperon, to Paris, where she enrolled at the renowned Music Conservatory. Her teacher and mentor,

the highly-esteemed Monsieur Lambert and his wife invited her to reside with them in their spacious apartment, in close vicinity to the Conservatory. At the advice of Madame Lambert, Sybil changed her last name from Sandstorm to the more alluring-sounding Sandstrom. Her debut recital was a triumph and resulted in her being asked by some of the most well-known composers of the day to perform music they recently composed, some of it expressly for her voice. With her talent and beauty, Sybil became an overnight celebrity and her name was now mentioned in one breath with the likes of Sarah Bernhard, the Scottish opera diva Mary Garden and the notorious American-born beauty, known through her famous portrait as "Madam X." Paris was the center of culture and art and Sybil had become an important and prominent figure in it. Admired and courted by some of the most successful and influential men of the time, Sybil declined any such advances, asserting she was committed to live for her art alone.

On board the luxurious SS France, she was now traveling to the French speaking city in Louisiana, where she was to share her talent with her fellow Americans who, with great expectations, were waiting to see and hear her on the stage as Manon Lescaut: the young woman whose early greed and vanity turn into finding true love and eventually, a tragic end in the wilderness of the Louisiana desert coast.

Elaborate preparations were made in advance for her arrival. She was a famous star, not only among the opera lovers, but known to the general public as well. Sybil was by now a household name, her voice and beauty second to none, and all her performances were sold out in advance. A large crowd of fans and photographers gathered at the pier to welcome her upon arrival at the port.

Opening night finally arrived. The promenade leading to the theatre was brilliantly lit by golden-hued gas lamps and the arriving audience was a spectacle of glamour, elegance and style. The wealthy took their seats in the private boxes as well as the lively ticket holders in the upper gallery, all considering themselves fortunate to be present at the performance of the famed soprano.

As the house lights were dimmed, the open conversations turned to whispers, and in the orchestra pit, the tall and slender conductor was now a dark, birdlike silhouette, impatiently flapping his coattails, then lifting his long sinuous arms decisively while stiffening his posture in preparation for the overture. When the curtain was raised, all eyes were transfixed on the stage, awaiting Sybil's entrance. When the musical cue for Manon's first appearance was finally heard, the entire audience held its breath in anticipation, but to everyone's great surprise, the stage remained empty under the spotlight. The opera star was nowhere to be seen. The conductor dropped his arms to the side and as the orchestra stopped playing, gasps of apprehension were heard throughout the auditorium. Everyone was aghast and a feeling of worry hovered over the silent auditorium. The conductor abruptly left his podium and dashed through the backstage labyrinth of corridors to Sybil's dressing room. He found her sobbing as a flood of tears turned her theatrical makeup of white powder and red lipstick into a grotesque and frightening mask.

Relieved to find her in the theatre, the anxious conductor quickly realized that Sybil was in a state of panic. As he attempted to calm her down, she tried to explain the reason for her distress. "In a dream I had last night," she said in agitation, "a woman whose piercing eyes stared at me through the blazing red scarf she covered her head with, came near me, and in a dark tone of premonition said to me: 'Singing Manon tonight would be a grave mistake. Although it will be a great theatrical success for you, it would also be your very last performance'."

Understandably, having been so emotionally shaken, Sybil was now reluctant and afraid to put the dream to the test. She had already heard that the Southern city was a place where superstitions, dark secrets and fortune-telling abound. She could not bring herself to go on stage. The conductor was at a loss how to get the frightened Prima Donna to appear in front of the waiting audience in the sold out theatre. The Opera House could not possibly sustain the disastrous financial losses that would result from her refusal to appear. It suddenly occurred to him that her superstitious nature might as well be the solution to the looming crisis. "Wait in your dressing room until I come back with good news," he said to Sybil. He returned shortly, accompanied by a striking looking woman of raven-black hair and piercing eyes. While holding that woman's hand tight, in a tone full of confident grandiosity, he said to Sybil: "This woman's name is Zenaida. She is the most compelling and trusted fortune-teller in the Deep South." Through her tears, Sybil could not see the prankish wink he shared with the woman he brought along. Cunningly narrowing her eyes, the woman called Zenaida came close to look deep into Sybil's eyes and, in a melodious and most persuasive tone of voice, said to her: "Not singing on opening night is an evil and deceitful scheme of a jealous rival of yours. Tonight's performance will be the pinnacle of your career and will ensure many future glorious performances and high points in your life, on and off the stage." With a sudden change in her voice to a sharply articulated and imperious tone, she exclaimed, while at the same time wiping Sybil's tears and nimbly redoing her makeup: "Sybil must sing tonight! SO I, THE GREAT ZENAIDA, COMMANDS!" concluded with grand, flamboyant theatrical gestures. Sybil's eyes lit up and a child's smile replaced her tears. That night, Sybil's portrayal of Manon was an artistic triumph.

Through the long line of admirers waiting outside her dressing room, Sybil spotted the bold red scarf and the eyes she had seen in her dream. "Those are the eyes I will never forget," a flash of recognition crossed her mind. "When I was at the height of my career," said the woman to her, "I was sure that no other voice could ever surpass mine in beauty, and even if it did, I would have done anything, out of jealousy, to stop it from being heard. But a voice like yours cannot be stopped. Tonight, my jealousy turned into love and admiration." Sybil felt a chill passing through her body. She knew she was facing Gloria Olsen, the famed and haughty Canadian soprano of whose presence in the audience she was notified of ahead. It was known that Gloria Olsen had lost her voice after an unhappy and scandalous love affair and was no longer performing. She traveled though, all the way from Toronto to hear Sybil after having had read reports of her prodigious talent. Sybil was moved and happy at the strange encounter with the unknown woman that initially appeared to her in her dark dream and was concluded by meeting her in person and being blessed by her with prospects of happiness and success.

In the carriage back to her hotel, Sybil's thoughts were centered on the evening's events. She smiled as it suddenly dawned on her that the woman named Zenaida who had been introduced to her as a fortune-teller looked familiar as she recognized her later on the stage as a member of the chorus. Dressed in costume, she was summoned to the rescue by the quick-witted conductor and by convincing Sybil to perform acted brilliantly to redeem the evening's near-calamity.

The next day, on board the SS France, Sybil was on her way back to Paris. That evening, standing alone on the deck under the starry sky, she reflected back on the last few day's events. Dressed in a shimmering deep green and blue satin-silk evening gown and a cashmere shawl over her finely defined shoulders, she looked like she stepped out of a French oil painting. Looking thoughtfully out to the sea while the band was playing a melodious waltz, she heard a pleasant manly voice whispering close behind her neck: "Would you dance with me?" She turned to see a handsome gentleman with the warmest and most irresistible smile she had ever seen. She smiled back. While they danced, Sybil was in a daze. At dawn, they were still together on the deck watching the sunrise. When the ship arrived at the French port of Le Havre, the two disembarked, hand in hand, looking forward to a bright future together.

Zenaida's prediction, fortune-teller or not, came true to everyone's satisfaction.

BRUNA MEETS TOSCA AT THE NATIONAL THEATRE

Premiered at the Teatro dell'Opera in Rome in 1900, Puccini's Tosca is a suspenseful tale of politics and intrigue swirling around a famous diva as she tries to free her lover from a tyrannical police chief.

The year is 1924. Dark days loomed over Italy as the relentless grip of a ruthless and all-powerful tyrant strengthened.

A new, and much talked about production of Puccini's *Tosca* is to be performed tonight on the great stage of the National Opera Theatre. Endorsed by the authorities, the plot gets a new interpretation as it strives to justify their totalitarian and oppressive power. Starring as Tosca is the leading soprano and crowned Prima Donna, Bruna Ferrari. A fiery performer and an intensely strong woman, she is the favored singer of the ruling members of the regime and is supported by the committee that censures and controls the Opera House's productions as well. They will all be present at the performance and witness Bruna Ferrari's realistic and highly anticipated interpretation of Tosca. On her way to the theatre's stage door, she is walking alone in the narrow cobblestone alley, deeply immersing herself in the events and thoughts she needs to make the role her own.

Much like the onstage opera's heroine, Bruna is deeply in love with a young artist and an idealistic and noble-minded freedom-fighter named Vittorio Lombardi. He has secretly joined the underground resistance movement in order to defy the oppressive ruler and his corrupt political allies in the secret police. At the same time, Vittorio is employed as a set designer at the National Theatre where he and Bruna met. Bruna is caught in a predicament and shudders at the thought of what might happen should Vittorio's underground activities be discovered. Should their affair become known to the authorities, not only the future of her career would be in question, but both hers and her lover's lives would be in serious danger. She is vigilantly on-guard, willing to do and sacrifice anything she can in order to protect the man she loves and their future life together. Ironically, as she portrays Tosca, Bruna Ferrari is telling her own personal story.

She arrives at the stage door under a cloud of unease. She has not been comfortable with the excessive personal attention she has recently received from the dictatorial and newly-appointed manager of the theatre, Signor Pasquale Romani. A large and heavy-set man, he wears a long dark cloak, a black fedora hat and sports diamond-studded rings on each of his thick, nail polished fingers. He leaves behind him a heavy trail of a musky cologne blended with old sweat odor. Bruna Ferrari is not eager to meet him at the door. As she enters her dressing room, a strange feeling is taking over her. She can tell that someone has been there prior to her entrance.

Sitting down at her makeup dresser, she sees a dozen red roses and an official looking envelope on which the initials P.R. are printed in a grandiose fashion. She is distressed and filled with a sense of foreboding, but in an effort to downplay her concerns she tends to her pre-performance preparation, alas, her heart and mind are troubled. Holding her breath, she nervously tears the envelope open to find a note that reads: "I will be coming to see you at your dressing room this evening to wish you well before you go on stage," signed: Pasquale Romani. The stationary paper seems to have been almost torn under the pressure of the ink. Bruna is aware of his intentions and is filled with dread thinking of the presence of the man she intensely disdains.

An abrupt and heavy-handed knock on the door causes Bruna to nervously jump in her seat and cruelly reminds her that trouble is near. Without waiting for an answer, the large size Romani enters the room, sweaty, his heavy breath betrays the stench of a stale cigar. He walks towards her and, in a stentorian tone of voice, tells her that his own Castagna Mercedes automobile would be waiting for her immediately following the performance and will whisk her from the theatre to his Villa Boca residence in the posh Aventino section of town. "There, over dinner and wine, we shall discuss the future of your brilliant career," he tells her. Outwardly, his invitation appears to be complimentary and generous, but Bruna clearly recognizes the hardly-disguised underlying threats and their implications. She knows all too well that

she has no choice but to accept, and that she is heading for a dead-end crisis.

As she exits the stage door after the evening's performance, the shiny black and sleek looking car is already waiting for her with its headlights blinking with glaring flashes like a police car. Wrapped in a shawl to protect her vocal cords, Bruna is helped into the back seat politely, and with subtle firmness, by the young and handsome chauffer, wearing dark glasses and a leather jacket, who introduces himself as Dino, Signor Pasquale Romani's private driver and security guard. Bruna cannot help wonder whether he is aware that she is studying his face through the front mirror. As Dino turns the luxury car engine on, the radio is turned on as well, broadcasting the revolting and endless populist demagogy of the abhorred dictator. Bruna Ferrari is on edge. She is filled with terror, knowing that she is trapped in a no-win situation. She keeps her face as calm as she can, and being the devout woman she is, prays silently.

At the dinner table, Romani does not waste time before telling her that he has the power to make her the most successful opera star in Italy should she become his lover. Repulsed, she also knows that he is a ruthless and power-hungry man with close ties to the state police who, in no time, would arrest and torture her Vittorio. Her mind is racing. She is frantic and asks him for one more performance before giving in to his advances. With a dubious smirk on his face, he agrees.

It is in the following evening's performance of Act 2's powerful scene when Tosca is facing Baron Scarpia, the cruel and corrupt chief of police. He demands her favors while the man she loves, Mario, is heard being tortured in the antechamber. Tosca pleads for mercy, but to no avail. The cruel Scarpia is using her anguish to extort his wishes and seems to enjoy the situation. Tosca is enraged and is about to stab him with the dinner knife she is hiding behind her back. At that point, while performing on the stage, Bruna sees the detested theatre manager Romani in the wings, he, being unseen by the audience, openly eyeing her with greed and lust. Bruna is experiencing Tosca's fury along with her own, personal fear and frustration. Walking on stage towards Scarpia, she spots a flashy pair of steel scissors, apparently left in a hurry on the floor by the stage-hand during scenery change. Bruna is certain it was fatefully predestined to be there for her, and decisively picks it up. She holds and stares at it glaringly, a strange smile on her face, she then lifts her head up, looks up to heaven and makes the sign of the cross. She then abruptly changes stage directions while the baffled onstage target Scarpia, looking bewildered, is heard through the auditorium, yelling: "Bruna, where on earth are you going?" She quickly turns away from him and runs instead, as fast as she can towards the wings where, with the deadly scissors already pointed towards him, she stabs the despised Romani in his chest. She returns, breathless, to center stage. Her hands drip blood. She laughs triumphantly, repeatedly hitting the very highest notes of her dramatic soprano. The audience is ecstatic, shouting "Brava Bruna" over and over. The bleeding Romani makes his way on his knees crawling unto the stage, scissors dug in his chest, and faithful to the opera script, he shouts: "Socorrso! Aiuto" ("Help! Help!") as he collapses dead while Bruna follows the opera script she knows so well, shouting: "Muori! Muori! Muori!" ("Die, Die, Die"), all in full view of the audience.

Under a spell, the audience is honoring Bruna with a standing ovation. The thundering "bravos" overcome the piercing sound of the police sirens already waiting for the last applause.

After repeated curtain calls, the audience leaves the theatre shocked but impressed by the unexpected and authentic ending of the opera's new production. Bruna leaves the theatre's door to receive one last standing ovation from the two young officers as she is escorted into the police car.

No one has ever played Tosca better than Bruna Ferrari at her final and legendary performance at the National Theatre.

CARMEN IN ALABAMA

Composed by George Bizet in 1875, Carmen tells the downfall of a young soldier named Don Jose who is enticed and seduced by the manipulations of the impulsive and unpredictable gypsy Carmen.

In her early years, when she was still a schoolgirl, Camila Richardson had already shown great musical promise, singing with the choir of the Baptist church in the little, quaint and peaceful southern town of Somerville, Alabama. Her angelic voice and gentle demeanor were always a comforting and loving presence to all who heard her sing with passion and devotion, though having been raised by her fervently devout grandmother, anyone's attempt to know Camila more closely was always met with an air of polite, yet firmly guarded disposition.

Recognizing her exceptional musical gift, the church parishioners raised the funds needed to send her to the big city on a scholarship for further training. Camila left for Chicago to study with Tony Marcelo, master teacher and mentor to many famous singers of the day. Living arrangements were made for her to reside with and be part of the household in the Reverend John H. Allensworth's family. Unfailingly, Camila sang at every Sunday service at the Central Baptist Church, and resolutely kept her roots in the service of her faith. In time, her pure-sounding voice, passion for music and hard work, along with Maestro Marcelo's expert guidance, led her on the way to embark on a rising career as a lyric soprano. Invited to sing leading roles at the most prestigious Opera Houses in the country, she remained humble and grateful. Camila was unswervingly committed to her steadfast belief that her God-given talent was intended to serve a heavenly mission, her voice a vessel through which people's connection with the divine would be strengthened. "Singing is a calling assigned to you by the Holy Spirit," pastor Allensworth told her.

Traveling back to Somerville on an overnight train, Camila was happy to pay a visit to her small town where she was to sing the role of Michaela: A shy and innocent girl who is in search of her childhood friend, a handsome soldier named Don Jose with whom she is secretly in love. Crossing a perilous rugged terrain, she finds him and hopelessly tries to persuade him to turn away from the dangerous Carmen and return to his home where his old mother is waiting for him.

Through the long overnight journey, Camila's thoughts went back to her earlier years. Somerville had never left her heart and neither had Donald Spencer, a young man she knew from her school days. The years that passed had not diminished the passion she had always felt for him and one that

she had always kept hidden. She realized and admitted to herself that seeing him again was indeed the true reason for her return to Somerville.

Camila arrived at Somerville's small station in the early morning. With her grandmother already gone to heaven, she walked alone to the small inn she was to be staying at while in Somerville.

Sitting at the inn's breakfast room the next morning, Camila, in a casual and off-handed air, inquired with Grace, the old innkeeper she knew, whether Donald Spencer was still living in Somerville. As she learnt that he now was involved with a woman named Tyra Jones, Camila's heart sank. Ms. Grace told her: "A woman of questionable character, Tyra Jones showed up in Somerville one day and found work at the local bar, where owing to her bold behavior and daring dancing abilities, she became popular with all the regulars who frequented the establishment. Donald Spencer was one of them and was now hopelessly in love with her." Upon hearing that, Camila felt a sudden pain in her chest while Ms. Grace continued: "No one in Somerville knows much of Tyra Jones' past life. It is believed that she was born across the border in Mexico where her parents abandoned her soon after birth. The baby girl was found at the doorsteps of the Catholic church and was then placed in a shelter for deserted children. At age 10, she was admitted to a girls' school at a convent. Not amenable to the disciplinary education, she escaped and grew up alone in the streets of a nearby town where she learnt to fend for herself. She now lives in a room in a run-down motel and comes and goes as she pleases." After hearing Grace, Camila sensed old and strangely familiar sadness sinking into her heart. She felt torn between hope, fear and hurt. The man she adored and the one she was hoping to connect with, was now tied up with another woman, the seductive and troublesome Tyra.

By now a well-known performer of high reputation, Camila had to focus, in spite of her distress, on the final dress rehearsal to be taking place the next day. After all, Carmen was the most talked about event in Somerville and she had the moral responsibility to meet the town's people expectations, taking into account the great efforts they had all made to make it happen: The orchestra was assembled from volunteers as was the small chorus. The costumes were sewn by the church's women's club and the sets consisted of backdrops painted by students of the high school's art class. The conductor was a young man studying at the local music college, modestly paid yet happy and eager to be given the opportunity to gain experience. Camila donated her fee as a gift to her church where she had first experienced her great love for singing and was given her first opportunity to be heard by an audience.

"Carmen" was to be performed on Sunday afternoon. That morning, Camila rose up early and entered the church before the service was to begin. She wanted to be alone in the chapel. She knelt and quietly prayed for Donald Spencer and her love for him. She then stood up and sang the "Pass Me Not Oh Gentle Savior" the way she used to sing it with the church's choir. Tears came down her face. They were tears of gratitude for the gift she was given to share with her people and the world, and they were tears of grace for the love she was still holding for the man she knew. She then headed to the theatre in order to become more familiar with its stage and the sound response in the small auditorium.

When she was done, Camila left the theatre and crossed the village-green to get back to her room in the inn. Grace, the innkeeper, looked troubled. "Donald Spencer got into a fight and was injured in a brawl when Tyra Jones had been seen with another man," she said gravely and without being asked, as if she knew what was on Camila's mind. Silently, Camila proceeded to her room, feeling heavy-hearted and somewhat angry. She did not deserve this unsettling news just before her performance. She needed peace.

Hours later, Camila was a radiant and lovable Michaela on the stage of the Somerville Opera House where every single seat was taken by the enthusiastic audience. Don Jose, the man she loved in her onstage role, was sung by Daryl Goodwin, a young and promising tenor studying at the prestigious music academy in Philadelphia. On stage Don Jose is indifferent to Michaela, but Daryl Goodwin has already fallen in love with Camila Richardson.

Leaving the theatre after the outstanding performance, Camila and Daryl, walking together, heard a loud noise coming from a commotion happening nearby, right by the Town Hall's door. Police cars were everywhere. Camila's heart was filled with a sense of foreboding. Camila and Daryl were told that a man named Donald Spencer had just shot a woman named Tyra Jones and was arrested. Daryl Goodwin was not aware that Camila knew Donald Spencer. He gently and protectively put his arms around her shoulders. Camila closed her eyes, took a deep breath and opened her eyes to find Daryl looking at her, smiling tenderly. Camila's heart was calm again. She felt safe.

Camila never saw Donald Spencer again. She did not need to as her heart was now free and open to receive the love that was waiting for her, and the one that she deserved.

ABOUT THE AUTHOR

Chaim Freiberg had a long and distinguished career performing, teaching and composing music. Chaim was twice honored by the Kaufman Music Center in New York City, in recognition of his outstanding work in the field of piano pedagogy with children.

Chaim Freiberg holds degrees from the Rubin Academy of Music, Tel-Aviv and The Juilliard School, New York City. He lives in the lovely city of Saint Petersburg, Florida, where he shares quality time with friends and the enchanting Boston terrier, Asia.

This collection of stories is a continuation of Chaim's affinity, as with the previously published "Ms. Adelaide's Piano", to connect with the creative soul and will be enjoyed by the young, as well as the adult reader.

PRAISE FOR MS. ADELAIDE'S PIANO

"Utterly enchanting"
Julia Cameron, bestselling author

"You pull back a curtain and allow your readers to look into your soul."
Robert Petterson, author of "Book Of Amazing Stories."

"A beautiful, diamond-faceted story cut with precision. I was mesmerized."
Avital Ronell, Professor of German and Comparative Literature, New York University.

"Some of the stories are striking and offer beautiful introspection."
Readers Digest Book Award competition.

www.ingramcontent.com/pod-product-compliance
Lightning Source LLC
Chambersburg PA
CBHW081127300726
48982CB00005B/873